GET READY...GET SET...READ!

THE
PANCAKE DAY

by
Foster & Erickson

Illustrations by
Kerri Gifford

BARRON'S

"It's light outside.
Wake up, Jake!" said Blake.

"It is Pancake Day.
Who will eat the most?"

"No more sleep, Jake.
You must keep awake."

"We think you can eat
the most pancakes."

"There are Flute and Sue.
Oh look, Rose came too."

"There are KC and Caroline.
And behind them
is Little Porcupine."

"Oh my dear," said Flute.
"What are you doing here?"

"This must be a joke,"
she said with a poke.

"If you are BIG and WIDE
you can put more food inside."

"Yes, being big is divine,"
said KC and Caroline Swine.

"Look at me, look at KC,
look at Caroline and Sue."

"My dear, even Rose
is bigger than you."

"Run along now and play,"
said Flute.

"I am little, but I will stay.
When it comes to pancakes,
I can put them away."

"I suppose I must show you
what BIG and WIDE can do."

"Let's show him how much
we can drink, Sue."

With noses like hoses,
they began to drink.

"Yes, drinks would be fine,"
said KC and Caroline Swine.

"Here goes," said Rose.

They all showed Porcupine
how much they could drink.

When the pancakes came,
the BIG and the WIDE
could not eat much.

They were all full inside.

Jake would not wake.
He did not eat
even one pancake.

After all the fun,
Rose could only eat one.

Blake had two
and so did Sue.

Caroline and KC
could only eat three.

Flute ate four,
but could eat no more.

Today, **little** was better.
Yes, little was fine.

Little Porcupine ate nine!

DEAR PARENTS AND EDUCATORS:

Welcome to **Get Ready...Get Set...Read!**

We've created these books to introduce children to the magic of reading.

Each story in the series is built around one or two word families. For example, *A Mop for Pop* uses the OP word family. Letters and letter blends are added to OP to form words such as TOP, LOP, and STOP.

This **Bring-It-All-Together** book serves as a reading review. *The Pancake Day* uses the characters and words introduced in SET 3. When your children have finished *Jake and the Snake*, *Jeepers Creepers*, *Two Fine Swine*, *What Rose Does Not Know*, and *Pink and Blue*, it is time to have them read this book.

Bring-It-All-Together books provide:
• much needed vocabulary repetition for developing fluency.
• longer stories for increasing reading attention spans.
• new stories with familiar characters for motivating young readers.

We have created this **Bring-It-All-Together** book to help develop confidence and competence in your young reader. We wish you much success in your reading adventures.

Kelli C. Foster, Ph.D.
Educational Psychologist

Gina Clegg Erickson, MA
Reading Specialist

All inquiries should be addressed to:
Barron's Educational Series, Inc.
250 Wireless Boulevard
Hauppauge, NY 11788

International Standard Book Number 0-8120-1055-8
Library of Congress Catalog Card Number: 94-74159

PRINTED IN CHINA
19 18 17 16 15 14 13 12 11 10

3 1333 03922 9404

There are five sets of books in the

Series. Each set consists of five **FIRST BOOKS** and two **BRING-IT-ALL-TOGETHER BOOKS**.

SET 1

is the first set your children should read.
The word families are selected from the short vowel sounds:
at, **ed**, **ish** and **im**, **op**, **ug**.

SET 2

provides more practice
with short vowel sounds:
an and **and**, **et**, **ip**, **og**, **ub**.

SET 3

focuses on
long vowel sounds:
ake, **eep**, **ide** and **ine**, **oke** and **ose**, **ue** and **ute**.

SET 4

introduces the idea that the word family sounds
can be spelled two different ways:
ale/ail, **een/ean**, **ight/ite**, **ote/oat**, **oon/une**.

SET 5

acquaints children with word families that
do not follow the rules for long and short vowel sounds:
all, **ound**, **y**, **ow**, **ew**.